ROB CHILDS

THE BIG WIN

Illustrated by Aidan Potts

YOUNG CORGI BOOKS

THE BIG WIN
A YOUNG CORGI BOOK: 0 552 545325

First published in Great Britain

PRINTING HISTORY
Young Corgi edition published 1998

3 5 7 9 10 8 6 4 2

Set in 14/18pt Linotype New Century Schoolbook by
Phoenix Typesetting, Ilkley, West Yorkshire.

Young Corgi Books are published by Transworld Publishers Ltd,
61–63 Uxbridge Road, Ealing, London W5 5SA,
in Australia by Transworld Publishers,
c/o Random House Australia Pty Ltd,
20 Alfred Street, Milsons Point, NSW 2061,
in New Zealand by Transworld Publishers,
c/o Random House New Zealand,
18 Poland Road, Glenfield, Auckland,
and in South Africa by Transworld Publishers,
c/o Random House (Pty) Ltd,
Endulini, 5a Jubilee Road, Parktown 2193

Made and printed in Great Britain by
Mackays of Chatham PLC, Chatham, Kent

It was from the corner that Langby deservedly went in front. Philip's head cleared the first cross, but only as far as the edge of the penalty area. Mark was daydreaming. He failed to pick up the attacker lurking there and made no attempt to block the shot. The ball was driven firmly through a ruck of bodies past the helpless Chris and into his net.

Mark looked down at his borrowed boots in dismay for a moment. But when he raised his head, the Danebridge players saw there was a silly grin spreading across his face.

'Oh, well, not to worry,' he said with a shrug. 'It's only a game. Who cares about losing when you're a millionaire?'

Also available by Rob Childs,
and published by Young Corgi Books:

THE BIG BREAK
THE BIG CHANCE
THE BIG CLASH
THE BIG DAY
THE BIG DROP
THE BIG FIX
THE BIG FREEZE

THE BIG GAME
THE BIG GOAL
THE BIG KICK
THE BIG MATCH
THE BIG PRIZE
THE BIG STAR
THE BIG WIN

Collections
THE BIG FOOTBALL COLLECTION
(includes The Big Game / The Big Match / The Big Prize)
THE BIG FOOTBALL FEAST
(includes The Big Day / The Big Kick / The Big Goal)

Coming soon:
THE BIG FOOTBALL TREBLE
(includes The Big Break/The Big Chance/The Big Star)

Published by Corgi Yearling Books:
SOCCER MAD
ALL GOALIES ARE CRAZY
FOOTBALL DAFT
FOOTBALL FANATIC
FOOTBALL FLUKES
SOCCER STARS
SOCCER MAD COLLECTION
(includes Soccer Mad / All Goalies are Crazy)
SOCCER AT SANDFORD
SANDFORD ON TOUR

Published by Corgi Pups,
for beginner readers:

GREAT SAVE!
GREAT SHOT!

*For all young footballers –
boys and girls!*

1 Winter Games

'Come on – run! Too cold to stand about. Find those spaces.'

The headmaster of Danebridge Primary School normally looked forward to taking the Year 5 Games lesson. Even on a bitter Monday afternoon in mid-January. But Mr Jones had something else on his mind today. He'd rather have been sitting behind his office desk next to the warm radiator.

'Huh! All right for old Jonesy,'

grunted Philip. 'Just look at him, all wrapped up in his thick coat and scarf.'

Chris grinned. 'Not to mention a weird, red bobble hat! Never seen him in that thing before.'

'Perhaps it was a Christmas present. Y'know, one of them yukky things from some aunt, like a jumper that's miles too big.'

They giggled. 'It'd have to be massive not to fit you,' said his pal.

Chris Weston was certainly pleased with his own presents. The school team captain was wearing his new soccer boots and his snazzy, green goalie gloves. He couldn't wait to give them their debut in tomorrow's league match, Danebridge's first game of the New Year.

'Get going, you two. No time to stop for a chat.'

Mr Jones had spotted them. Even with over thirty pupils dodging about inside the square training grids, anybody standing still shone out like a lighthouse. Especially someone Philip's height!

They darted once more into the crowd of hurtling bodies, swerving this way and that to try and avoid contact. The gangly centre-back, with his long thin legs, found it an almost impossible task. His accidental trip on a daydreaming passer-by was worthy of a yellow card!

'Soz, Kerry,' he apologized quickly. 'Are you OK?'

The girl scrambled to her feet. 'Yes — no thanks to you,' she snapped, angry at the dirty smear down the side of her new tracksuit. 'Just see what you've made me do. You're like a clumsy, baby giraffe.'

'Said I'm sorry, didn't I? You should've been looking where you were going.'

Before their argument could heat up further, Mr Jones blew his whistle and ordered the players into groups of four. 'Mixed,' he stressed. 'Don't spend long choosing, I'm not asking you to marry each other!'

Chris and Philip were joined reluctantly by Kerry and a friend as Mr

Jones continued to bark out instructions. 'Four-a-side games in the grids now – and no goalies. I want you all on the move.'

For once, Danebridge's keeper didn't mind about the ban on goalies. He'd injured a hand during the holidays at an indoor soccer tournament and he wasn't going to risk hurting his fingers again before the match.

Chris turned to Kerry. 'Me and Phil can be the defence while you two stay up in attack. How about that?'

'Suits me,' said Kerry with a shrug. 'I like scoring goals.'

'I know. I keep saying you should come and play for the school team.'

She shook her head. 'I go riding Saturday mornings.'

'Not all our games are on Saturdays. Like tomorrow, for instance.'

'Yeah, two-thirty kick-off, away,' Philip grinned. 'We're missing most of afternoon school.'

'Still not for me,' she said. 'I'll stick to horses and netball.'

'Pity!' Chris sighed. 'We need a good goalscorer.'

That was true. Danebridge had picked up after a poor start to the season, but they were still finding goals hard to come by. Rakesh Patel in Year 6 was their leading scorer, but he'd only found the net four times.

Kerry immediately showed her eye for goal. Less than a minute into the game, she gave her marker the slip and stroked the ball clean through the centre of the narrow, coned target.

Chris whistled under his breath. 'Magic! I've got to change her mind about playing for us somehow. She's deadly!'

Kerry proved too much of a handful for anybody to keep under control on such a small pitch. Her speed off the mark allowed her to reach a pass with time and space to shoot before a defender could make a challenge. Their opponents even stopped trying after she notched up a hat-trick.

'Great stuff, Kerry!' Philip applauded her. 'If I'm a baby giraffe, you're making this lot look like wooden donkeys!'

The teams soon swapped round, forming different foursomes for another game. Chris now discovered for himself just how difficult it could be to play against her. Kerry seemed to delight in showing up the limitations of the school captain when he had the ball at his feet and not in his hands. It was an uncomfortable experience.

His most embarrassing moment came when he delayed too long on the ball before passing it. Kerry whipped it off his toes, but he recovered enough to block her route to goal and make her nearly run the ball out of play. Chris thought he had Kerry trapped on the touchline, but it was wishful thinking. She cheekily knocked the ball through his legs, nipped round him to regain possession and then coolly sidefooted it in.

Chris greeted the headmaster's shrill whistle with some relief. Mr Jones had decided to cut the session short and ushered everyone back inside to thaw out. Nobody complained, not even the keenest of footballers.

'Brrr! Hope it's not so cold tomorrow,' said Chris, crouched against the radiator in the boys' cloakroom. 'I'll freeze to death in goal.'

'Depends how busy you are,' smiled Philip. 'Langby School are near the top of the league, so I doubt if you'll have a chance to get frostbite!'

As the bell rang for home-time, Rakesh burst into the cloakroom.

'Hey!' he yelled out in excitement. 'You guys heard the big news about Mark Towers?'

'Only that he's away today,' muttered Chris, regretting that Mark might have to miss the match. 'What's so big about that? We can manage without him.'

'Our teacher's just told us why he's away,' Rakesh grinned, barely able to contain himself. 'His family have gone and won the National Lottery!'

2 It Could Be You!

Chris lay in bed that night, unable to sleep. The street light cast flickering shadows into the room he shared with Andrew, his elder brother, who'd left the primary school the year before. They were both thinking about the same thing.

'You still awake?' he hissed across the room.

'No,' Andrew yawned.

'What would *you* do if you'd won all that money?'

'Spend it.'

'What on?'

'Football gear. For a start, I'd buy all United's latest strips, plus expensive boots and trainers. Dead flash, like – only the best. Could wear a different pair every day if I wanted to.'

'C'mon, be serious. You can't blow it all on boots and kit.'

'Well, I'd also need a season ticket to sit in one of United's plush executive boxes. Might even buy them a new player. Mind you, can't get anybody decent for only a million or so these days.'

'There *are* other things in life besides football, you know.'

'Not much at our age,' Andrew grumbled. 'No point buying a car – can't drive. Too young to go off round the world. Mum wouldn't let me.'

'OK, OK, if you're just going to be silly. Might as well try to get to sleep. G'night.'

Andrew was quiet for a while, then said, 'Tell you something, our kid.'

'What?'

'Don't reckon I'd like to be a millionaire after all.'

'Why not?'

'Well, as Grandad said earlier to

me, you wouldn't know who your real friends are.'

'How d'yer mean?'

'You'd always be wondering which they liked best – you or your money! G'night, little brother.'

'This is going to be one of those days,' sighed Mr Jones as he drove into Danebridge the following morning. 'I can feel it in my bones.'

He was right. Tuesday began badly and steadily got worse. He even had to abandon school assembly because the children were so noisy and excited. A strange kind of fever seemed to have come over them, but its symptoms were all too obvious – wide eyes, shaking heads and green faces.

The headmaster hadn't needed to consult a medical dictionary, however, for the cause of the bug. Its name was jealousy.

Mark had turned up at school unexpectedly and was clearly revelling in his new-found fame. He'd already been heard on local radio the previous evening after rumours of the family's good fortune in the weekend Lottery draw had spread beyond the village.

'How does it feel to be so rich at your age, Mark?' he was asked during the interview.

'Real cool.'

'Is it true that you chose the lucky numbers?'

'Yes, but they're special, not lucky,' he corrected the reporter, pleased to have the chance to show off his mathe-

matical knowledge. 'We always have them. They're the first six square numbers – 4, 9, 16, 25, 36 and 49. That's not counting number one, of course.'

'Of course,' the woman repeated, not wishing to admit that she had no idea what the boy was talking about. She'd quickly moved on to ask his parents whether they were going to give up working.

Mr Jones was worried that the same question might also apply to his pupils. Very little work was being done at school due to the effects of this Lottery fever, especially in Mark's class. The children simply weren't able to concentrate.

Mark found himself surrounded in the playground at morning break by a large group of grinning admirers. They all knew who he was, even if he couldn't put a name to most of them.

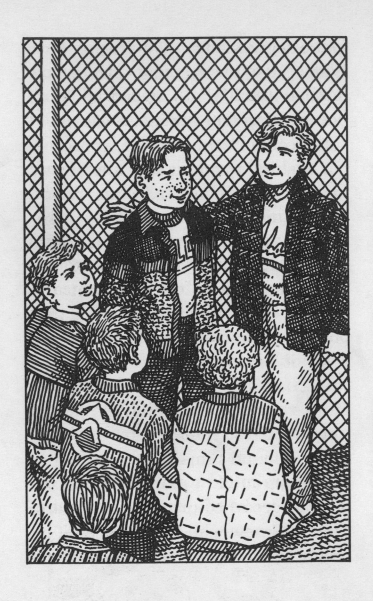

Close by his side, though, was Paul Walker, a fellow member of the school football team. Paul appeared quite happy to confess his ignorance about square numbers.

'Don't tell me *you* don't know what they are either,' Mark scoffed. 'We did them again in class last term.'

'I'm no good at maths,' Paul laughed. 'Not like you, Professor.'

It wasn't only Mark's brilliance at maths which had earned him that particular nickname. He was hopelessly absent-minded. Even on the soccer pitch he was liable to wander out of position as his attention drifted away from the game onto something clsc.

'They're called square numbers 'cos you can make square patterns out of

them,' Mark explained proudly to the whole group. 'Like four is two rows of two, and nine is made up of three rows of three – and so on.'

'If these numbers are so famous,' piped up a younger boy, 'lots of other people must have picked them too.'

'Not as many as you'd think. There were just five winning tickets.'

And then came the question that everybody kept asking. 'How much have you actually won?'

'Over two million pounds!' Mark boasted, enjoying the sound of all that money tripping off his tongue. 'Or to be precise – two million, three hundred and twenty thousand, four hundred and twelve pounds! That's only by my calculations, like, but I know I'm right.'

'Just listen to him,' groaned Philip as he and Chris passed by. 'He's

lapping up all this star treatment. Last week, everybody would have said the Professor was dead boring.'

'Yeah, but now he's dead boring with loadsamoney!' Chris said, recalling Andrew's remark. 'That's the difference.'

As always, Chris's grandad helped out with transport to the game that afternoon. He turned round to speak to his young passengers before they set off.

'If anyone mentions the Lottery on this journey, I'll make them get out and walk the rest of the way,' he promised with a wink.

'Just as well that Mark's in Jonesy's car, then,' Chris grinned.

'Aye, it is. I can't go anywhere

without hearing people going on about you-know-what. It's driving me mad.'

'Imagine what it's like for me, being in his class,' muttered Rakesh.

Chris shook his head in mock sympathy. 'You'll have to stick some cotton wool in your ears to shut him out.'

'Pardon?' his friend said, pretending to remove a piece, and then laughed. 'I don't think the Professor even knows what day it is. He's on another planet. He's got too many numbers flying around inside his head.'

'They must have plenty of space,' Philip put in. 'It's suddenly grown twice as big!'

'He'd forgotten all about this match, you know,' Rakesh told them. 'Jonesy's had to find a spare kit and kids were almost queuing up to lend him their boots.'

'Hardly surprising after what's happened. He never remembers to bring his own, anyway.'

Rakesh nodded. 'Yeah, but he usually has to go round *begging* people for a pair.'

'The Professor reckons his parents'

memories are even worse than his,'
Philip chuckled, shaking his head in
amazement. 'Trust a family like that
to have all the luck!'

'We might be better off without him,
the way he is at the moment,' said
Chris. 'I mean, on form, he does a good
job in midfield with his strong tackles
and that. But it'll probably be like
playing with ten men today.'

Grandad interrupted. 'I hope not.
It's going to need a really good team
performance to get a result against
Langby. You've all got to do your bit.'

The headmaster felt the same way.
But as he led the small convoy of cars
towards the market town of Langby,
Mr Jones doubted whether the boys
were in the right frame of mind to
play such an important football

match. With the temperatures still barely above freezing, he feared that Langby might catch them cold in more ways than one.

Another defeat could prove costly. Danebridge were still too close for comfort to the league's relegation zone . . .

3 Team Spirit

Chris found himself under bombardment straightaway.

When the ball was rolled to one side at the kick-off, a Langby player suddenly whacked it goalwards from well inside the centre-circle. He hoped to catch the Danebridge keeper off guard and off his line.

His plan almost worked too. As Chris desperately back-pedalled, the ball dropped from the sky out of his reach, bounced up high and sailed

less than a metre wide of the target. Chris heaved a huge sigh of relief.

'That's just a sighter,' laughed the home team captain. 'Welcome to Langby. We're the league's top scorers.'

Chris soon saw why. He faced a barrage of shots from all angles and distances and did well to keep Langby at bay for as long as ten minutes. His new gloves were now splattered with dirt, and a point-blank range blaster made his damaged fingers tingle as he touched it over the bar.

It was from the corner that Langby deservedly went in front. Philip's head cleared the first cross, but only as far as the edge of the penalty area. Mark was daydreaming. He failed to pick up the attacker lurking there and made no attempt to block the shot. The ball was driven firmly through a ruck of bodies past the helpless Chris and into his net.

Mark looked down at his borrowed boots in dismay for a moment. But when he raised his head, the Danebridge players saw there was a silly grin spreading across his face.

'Oh, well, not to worry,' he said with a shrug. 'It's only a game. Who cares about losing when you're a millionaire?'

'Come on, Mark Towers, get stuck in!' cried Mr Jones from the touchline as Danebridge restarted the game.

'They're just walking through us.'

It was obvious to everyone that Mark wasn't pulling his weight for the team. Out on the pitch, however, many of the players were letting him know rather more forcibly that they weren't exactly thrilled by his efforts.

'You're about as much use as a chocolate tea-pot!'

'You are allowed to move, you know. You're not nailed to the spot.'

Rakesh nudged into Mark as he jogged by, almost knocking him over.

'Out of the way. You're cluttering the place up, just standing there.'

'You did that on purpose,' Mark protested, glaring at Rakesh.

The winger feigned innocence. 'Why would I do a thing like that?'

'I could give you two million reasons.'

'Don't let them rile you, Mark,' said Paul, running up to him in support. 'They're just jealous, that's all.'

'They can say what they like,' he smirked. 'Doesn't bother me now.'

Chris couldn't get close enough to give Mark an earful, but Philip did his job for him. 'We'll have you off at half-time, Professor, if you don't start getting a few tackles in,' he warned.

Mark scowled. 'Right, you're another one who won't be having a sniff of any money when I dish some of it out to my friends.'

Class No. .... Acc. No. ....

'I don't want your money,' Philip sneered. 'I just want you to try and help us win this game.'

That was looking more and more of an unlikely prospect. Langby kept streaming forward, sweeping through the gaps in midfield that Mark should have been filling.

Langby were so much on top that it came as no surprise when they scored a second goal. It was an excellent solo strike by their skilful winger, whose burst of speed left Paul for dead. He

dummied his way past Philip, too, before unleashing a fierce shot beyond Chris's dive.

'I suppose you think that was Mark's fault as well, do you?' said Paul.

Philip bristled at the full-back's sarcasm. 'You're a creep, the way you keep sticking up for him all the time. I wonder why?'

'What d'yer mean by that?'

'Huh! Do I have to spell it out for you? Everybody knows why you're suddenly crawling round the Professor.'

Paul didn't take kindly to that remark either and it was a good thing that the captain managed to step between them in time.

'Cut it out, both of you, and get on with the game,' Chris said firmly.

'We've got no chance if we're falling out with each other. We're two-nil down already.'

Soon it was three. And this third goal was a real sickener for any hopes of staging a comeback. Mark finally stirred himself enough to join in the action and attempted to guide the ball back to Paul. His pass was weak and misdirected, giving the Langby captain a late Christmas present.

'Ta very much,' the boy cackled gratefully. But only after he'd tucked the ball away into the net.

Mr Jones was not amused. 'I could see this kind of sloppy display coming,' he fumed at half-time. 'You're just not with it, some of you.'

Mark gave a defiant shrug as the headmaster glanced his way. Nor did he endear himself to Mr Jones when his muttered comment was just a little too loud to ignore. 'I didn't want to come to school today in the first place. Don't see why I should have to any more.'

Mr Jones struggled to control his temper, but he knew this wasn't the right time or place to discipline the boy. For now, Mark was one of the three players substituted as he tried to reorganize his dispirited side. Paul and Philip were the others. The head-master had noted their argument and decided they could cool off by shivering together on the touchline. He'd deal with them – and Mark – later.

To their credit, Danebridge did make more of a fight of it in the second half. Without Mark's unsettling influence, they played far better as a team and managed to restrict Langby's goal-scoring chances. They even created some of their own too.

Rakesh went close with a shot that grazed the post and then he set substitute Ryan up for a goal on his debut. All Ryan had to do was tap the ball home after Rakesh's clever dribble down the wing pulled two defenders and the goalkeeper out of position. The young scorer's smile of pure delight briefly lit up a bleak afternoon for the visitors.

Sadly, things took a turn for the worse right at the end of the game with an injury to Chris. Langby broke clear in search of a fourth goal to clinch their victory and Chris dived bravely at the striker's feet to smother his shot. The ball ran loose for someone else to poke into the empty net and Chris was left on the ground, nursing his trampled fingers.

As the opposing captains shook hands at the final whistle, Chris was trying to hide the pain, both of the 4–1 defeat and also in his fingers. He was only glad he didn't have to shake with his left hand.

'Back home for some more first-aid,' Grandad said as Chris trudged off the field. 'Cup match on Saturday, remember, and we've got to have you fit to play in that.'

Chris grimaced. He hated the

thought of missing the cup-tie, but that wasn't the only problem on his mind. He'd just overheard Mark openly offering tempting bribes to several players to be friends with him again.

4 Who's in Goal?

Mark was absent from school the next day. Nor did his parents go into work. Neighbours reported that the family car stayed in the garage and callers found the curtains drawn and the doorbell unanswered. Even the phone was left off the hook.

If the strange disappearance of the Towers family was a mystery to people in the village, Danebridge's young footballers had more important matters to discuss. Still licking their wounds from the league defeat, they were wondering how they could avoid the same fate in the cup.

Chris's injury added to the worries. The captain was ever-present in goal and nobody else much fancied the job.

'Who's going to play there if you can't?' asked Philip.

'It could be you!' Chris grinned, shuffling forward in the lunch queue.

'I hope that was meant as a joke. C'mon, any ideas?'

Chris had already been giving the choice some serious thought and he was still none the wiser. 'Dunno really. Might have said Mark before, but I guess that's out of the question now. I don't suppose he'll be wanting to play for the school again. That's if he ever does come back here!'

'Don't reckon Jonesy would have him in the team anyway.'

Chris shrugged. 'Rakesh, maybe? He's OK.'

'Yeah, but we need him up front to knock one or two in for us.'

'That's been our main problem all season,' Chris sighed. 'Not being able to score more goals than the other team do!'

As if summoned by magic, Rakesh suddenly popped up to join them, jumping the queue. 'How's the hand?' he asked, ignoring complaints.

'Not too good. Hurts a bit when I hold anything.'

'Pity it's not your writing hand.'

Chris smiled. 'I'm still hoping it'll be OK for Saturday.'

'You could always play centre-forward,' Rakesh suggested, only half in jest. 'Might make a nice change, trying to put the ball into the net instead of keeping it out!'

'No, I'm rubbish on the pitch,' laughed Chris. 'At least that's what Andrew says.'

'Well, he would. At least it'd be better than biting your nails on the touchline, just watching.'

Chris held out his plate for ladled helpings of food from the hatches, taking extra care not to drop it. He added an apple and a drink to his tray and then looked around for some-where to sit. He spotted just the place. Right next to Kerry, the very person he wanted to talk to!

The following lunchtime was the soccer squad's regular Thursday training session while it remained too dark after school.

Mr Jones was keen to use it to give any volunteer goalkeepers some much needed practice – just in case. 'I won't name the team for the cup-tie until we see how Chris's hand feels tomorrow,' he explained, and then gave a grin. 'And I also want to check out our new signing here!'

All eyes turned towards the player in the red tracksuit.

'She can play in goal for us!' Rakesh piped up.

Kerry joined in the giggling. 'I'm

fine catching the ball in netball, but I don't think I'm ready to take Chris's place yet.'

'Why not? We could do a swap,' Rakesh smirked. 'Chris has always fancied playing netball!'

Jokes over, Kerry was soon impressing everyone with her shooting skills. Although Mr Jones was already well aware of the girl's ability, this was the first time an interested spectator had seen her in action.

Grandad was leaning on the fence that divided the playing field from a public footpath. He was the school's number one supporter. He rarely missed a match, home or away, and even liked to watch the footballers practise whenever he could.

Normally that was easy. He just had to wander down to the bottom of his garden to see them play on the village recreation ground behind his cottage. Their own playing field wasn't big enough for a full-size pitch. This lunchtime, however, he'd made the effort to come up to the school after Chris had told him about their new recruit.

'Aye, she's a good 'un, all right, no doubt about that,' he murmured to himself as Kerry cracked another shot into one of the small five-a-side goals.She can hit 'em with either foot.'

Several players had turns in the two goals, with the rest in groups waiting for a chance to shoot at them. To Grandad's experienced eye, none of the keepers on view could be chosen for the match with any confidence.

Chris came over to him during a short break in the practice. 'What do you reckon, then, Grandad?'

'About the goalies or the girl?'

'Both.'

'Well, m'boy,' he wheezed, blowing out his cheeks. 'I'd say that if you're not between the sticks, then Danebridge are in big trouble.'

Chris had expected Grandad to come out with something like that, but he still pulled a face. 'And Kerry? I'm surprised she actually agreed to play as it clashes with her horseriding. But she's worth the risk, eh?'

'What risk is that?'

'I deliberately got her mad at lunch yesterday,' he grinned. 'Said it was much harder to score a goal in a real match than just a kickabout in Games – and I bet her that she couldn't do it. Now she's out to prove me wrong.'

'So what happens if she does?'

His grin faded. 'I have to get up on top of a horse and jump a fence!'

Grandad nudged Chris on the arm to make him look round. Kerry was juggling a ball on her feet and knees, keeping it up in the air, just as Rakesh called out a playful challenge from the goal.

'C'mon, then, Kerry. Try and beat me. Bet you can't.'

She flicked the ball up a little

higher and as it dropped, struck it crisply on the half-volley. Rakesh dived in vain. He never even got close to the ball as it flashed past him into the corner of the net.

'It obviously doesn't pay to bet against this girl,' Grandad chuckled. 'Looks like you'll need to book some riding lessons, m'boy!'

5 Humble Pie

Mark arrived back at school on Friday morning, but village gossip reached the playground before him. The Towers hadn't won the Lottery after all. Their numbers had come up last week, but they'd forgotten to buy a ticket! It was said they only realized when they tried to claim their prize.

The Professor was greeted by jeers and taunts.

'Hey! Look who's here – it's the ex-millionaire!'

'You've got to be in to win!'

Mark glared at his tormentors. But his parents had warned him that he must not retaliate, no matter how bad any provocation might be. He sat alone in the headmaster's office while the junior classes were in assembly.

'Mark's going to need our help to get over all this business and put it behind him,' Mr Jones told his pupils. 'I know it's difficult, but try and forget that it ever happened. Just treat him like you used to before.'

As he returned to the office, Mr Jones felt like crossing his fingers. He could only hope that the children would respond in the right way. 'It was very brave of you to come to school today, Mark,' he said sympathetically. 'Not many would have done in your position.'

'Had to show up sometime,' sighed Mark. 'Mum and Dad left it to me.'

'Well, I think you may discover who your true friends are now at any rate,' Mr Jones said. 'Money can have a strange effect on people, you know. They can change – and not always for the better.'

Mark gulped, taking the point. 'Sorry about last Tuesday, Mr Jones. I hope you'll let me play again. That's why I'm here really.'

The headmaster nodded. 'I'm willing to forgive and forget, Mark, but it's your teammates that you need to apologize to as well.'

Mark was invited to the team meeting at breaktime and stood sheepishly in front of all the players. It was quite a shock for him to see Kerry sitting among them.

'I know I don't deserve another chance, the way I acted so stupid,' he began. 'I'm sorry. Just hope I'll be able to try and make up for it.'

Chris glanced round to check that others felt the same as he did. They were smiling. 'Nice to have the old Mark back,' the captain said. 'You could make a start tomorrow perhaps. How do you fancy playing in goal?'

Mark's jaw dropped. 'In . . . in goal! B . . . but . . .'

'No buts, Mark, I'm injured,' Chris insisted. 'Grandad's seen you play there in practice and rates you. And he should know, he used to be a keeper himself.'

'Yeah, he kept goal for Danebridge Prehistoric United!' giggled Rakesh.

'Well, don't mind where I play,' said Mark. 'If you really want me.'

'Sounds like that's already been decided,' said Mr Jones happily. 'No doubt Chris can lend you all the goalie kit you'll need – and maybe he could take your usual place in midfield. What do you say, Captain?'

Chris couldn't say anything. He was too flabbergasted. He'd never played out on the pitch in a match before in his life!

That evening at home, his brother was almost speechless too – only with laughter – when Chris gave him the team news.

'Glad my own game's been cancelled,' Andrew gasped out at last. 'I wouldn't miss watching this for the world. You in midfield and a girl in attack! Should be hilarious!'

'Don't you come along just to mock. I'm nervous enough as it is.'

'I just can't imagine a girl in a Danebridge shirt,' Andrew snorted in derision. 'Poor old Grandad will have a fit when he finds out.'

'He's already seen how Kerry can score goals. She's wicked!'

'I'll believe it when I see it with my own eyes. Reckon old Jonesy must be cracking up. I wouldn't trust the Professor in goal!'

'And you needn't go trying to put *him* off either during the match,' Chris warned. 'I shall have Grandad on guard duty behind the goal.'

'Never mind him being behind it. If Jonesy was so desperate, I'm surprised he didn't even ask Grandad to play in *front* of it tomorrow!'

In the changing hut on the recky next morning, Chris watched Mark pull on the school's green goalkeeping jersey and felt a sudden pang of resentment. He hadn't envied Mark his promised millions earlier in the week, but having the treasured top now was a different matter. Chris tended to regard it as his own property.

'Don't go playing *too* well, Professor,' he said, managing a smile. 'Remember it's only on loan for the day.'

Mark grinned and stepped into Rakesh's spare tracksuit bottoms. He'd forgotten to bring his own, of course. He also had to make do with the captain's old goalie gloves as Chris was still wearing his new ones. They helped him to feel less strange in a red and white striped shirt.

Chris clapped his gloves together to gain the players' attention before they left the hut. 'OK, men,' he began. 'This is the first round of the cup and we want . . .'

He paused, wondering why everyone was sniggering. Then he realized. Kerry was standing at the back of the group, hands on hips, giving him a hard stare. She had arrived at the hut fully changed and wasn't amused by having to wait outside in the cold until the boys were ready.

'Er . . . sorry, Kerry,' he faltered. 'OK, er . . . team, we want to turn it on today. The cup's our best hope of winning something this season.'

'Yeah, especially now we've missed out on the Lottery!' Mark piped up.

Only he could have got away with saying that in front of Mr Jones. The emergency keeper's joke at his own expense sent the team out in high spirits and their boots clattered down the wooden steps on to the grass.

The ground had fortunately soften-
ed up a little after the mid-week frost,
although the wind was still keen on
any bare flesh. Their opponents,
Brentway Juniors, were smartly
kitted out in royal blue, with
matching gloves, and Kerry immediately felt less conspicuous. She picked
out *two* girls in the Brentway line-up.

So had Andrew. 'There's more of
them!' he exclaimed, shaking his
head. 'What's the game coming to?'

Grandad chuckled. 'You'll have to
get used to it, m'boy. Young Kerry
may be the first girl to play soccer for
Danebridge, but she certainly won't
be the last.'

6 Goals Galore

Chris did not have the best of starts to the game. He lost the toss, let the ball go through his legs to a blue shirt in Brentway's first attack and then watched the girl's shot skid underneath Mark's late dive.

Fortunately for the captain, the ball veered past the wrong side of the post – the right side for Danebridge.

'Had it covered,' Mark claimed with a nervous grin.

Chris and Mark weren't the only

ones with early jitters. Other players were also guilty of uncharacteristic errors, perhaps still unsure about the reliability of their new keeper. Paul showed no confidence in him at all.

After Philip almost headed into his own net, Paul dithered on the ball in front of goal, panicked and gave it away. The free gift was hit hard and true and Mark barely saw it coming. He tried to duck out of the way of the missile, but it smacked him on the

back of his shoulder and spun up and out for a corner. He and Paul exchanged glares and a few words.

Things were little better in attack. Kerry sliced a good chance well wide of the target, staring after the ball in disbelief at her failure to score. And even Rakesh missed a sitter.

'C'mon, Reds!' cried Andrew from the touchline. 'Sort yourselves out. Show them who's boss of the recky!'

That was easier said than done. Brentway had already beaten Danebridge 2-1 at home in the league and now they were seeking a cup double. The visitors pressed hard for the opening goal, forcing Mark to fumble one shot and then deflect a sharp, close-range drive round the post.

'Well saved!' cried Chris, having to

play more in defence than midfield. 'Good job you *did* have that one covered! Would have gone in.'

'If there's one thing I'm good at, it's working out angles,' Mark replied. 'Reckon that was about a thirty degrees acute one. No way was I going to let it sneak in.'

Grandad was pleased too. 'Knew he'd be all right, that lad, once he settled down,' he said to himself. 'He'll be fine now.'

A goal came from the corner, but not for the attacking team. Chris blocked the ball in the six-yard box, Paul hacked it upfield, Kerry helped it on to Rakesh and Danebridge's leading scorer sprinted clear. This time he made no mistake. The break-away goal was against the run of play, but his teammates were not complaining about that.

By half-time, they were all smiles — even Paul. In a flurry of goals before the interval, Rakesh grabbed a second and Brentway responded with a header that Chris himself could not have kept out. But then Kerry stole the show.

She dispossessed one of the Brentway girls outside the area, but found her path to goal barred by two more defenders. She remained ice-cool, shielding the ball skilfully from challenges as she jockeyed for a better shooting position near the penalty spot.

Although passing never seemed to enter her head, Kerry still had her back to goal and looked in need of some help. Suddenly, without warning, she swivelled round and lashed a right-footed shot high into the top corner of the net.

The goalkeeper was left grasping at thin air, caught out by the speed of the strike. It was a moment of sheer class. One that gave proof that here was a natural goalmouth predator.

'Wow!' exclaimed Andrew, despite himself. 'Incredible! I didn't think she had space to do something like that.'

'Neither did they,' chuckled Grandad, looking at the shocked faces of the Brentway side as Danebridge celebrated.

'That's more like it,' Mr Jones encouraged them as the players gathered together at the break. 'You've just about earned this lead after a dodgy start. Three excellent goals and I'm sure there's more to come.'

He was right. Danebridge began the second half in determined fashion. Chris won the ball in the centre-circle, putting in the kind of

powerful tackle that his big brother might have been proud of. He stayed on his feet and sent Rakesh scampering away down the wing with a defence-splitting pass. The winger's cross was met perfectly by Ryan, brought on as substitute again, and he scored his second goal in two games.

There was no stopping Danebridge after that. The football traffic became one-way, streaming towards the Brentway goal like racing cars along the home straight in a Formula One Grand Prix.

Chris was even starting to enjoy himself in midfield. The captain had spent most of the game in his own half so far, battling away to try and break up the visitors' attacks, but now he felt able to join in the fun. Pushing forward deep into Brentway territory, he linked up neatly with Kerry in a move that ended with Rakesh completing his hat-trick.

Rakesh was running riot. He soon added a fourth to double his personal tally for the season, and then curled over a ball for the lanky Philip to climb above everybody else and head into the goal.

'Seven-one!' breathed Grandad. 'They're playing like millionaires!'

'I think you might have put that a bit better!' laughed Andrew, making Grandad redden slightly as he realized what he'd said.

Only once did Brentway manage to turn the tide and remind Mark that he was still playing in the match. On a rare raid, their left-winger swung an awkward cross into the goal-mouth, the ball swirling about in the wind. Mark adjusted his position, timed his jump well and caught the ball cleanly, showing a safe pair of hands.

As the opponents retreated, he allowed himself the luxury of bringing his feet into the action too. He dribbled the ball forward, well beyond his own penalty area, before finally hoofing it right into the other one.

The ball was only half-cleared by Brentway, bobbling loose in the box, and Kerry the killer pounced on her prey like a tigress. In a blink of an eye, the ball was nestling once more in the back of the net.

The visitors seemed to give up at last, overwhelmed by the onslaught, and the Danebridge captain put the icing on the cake. Chris, by his own admission, was not exactly 'Man of the Match' – if Kerry and the other girl players would accept such a term – but he deserved some reward for all his hard work. Rakesh was again the unselfish provider.

The winger could quite comfortably have scored a fifth himself, but he slipped the ball square instead to the unmarked Chris who had charged up in support of the attack. Chris hadn't anticipated a pass and for one awful moment, he thought the goalie was going to save his scuffed shot. The ball just trundled beyond his dive and clipped the post on its way in.

'About time, too,' Kerry laughed as Chris looked stunned by his goal. 'I thought you were going to leave all the scoring to us. I hope you've remembered our bet.'

'Giddy-up!' he whooped and slapped an imaginary horse before galloping all the way back to the halfway line. Only Grandad among the spectators could guess the reason for such a bizarre goal-celebration!

'C'mon, let's have double figures!' shouted Andrew, starting up a touch-line chant of 'We want ten!' from the younger supporters.

The team duly obliged. As Mr Jones checked his watch inside the final minute, he looked up to see the strange sight of a green top mixing with the red stripes on yet another Danebridge attack.

'Get back in goal,' Chris called out. 'What are you doing up here?'

'I'm bored!' Mark yelled. 'Got

nothing to do. I just wanted to have a run round and warm up a bit.'

His unexpected arrival in the opposition penalty area threw what was left of Brentway's defensive organization into total chaos. They had no idea who to mark.

Ryan lobbed the ball into the crowded goalmouth and it zigzagged about in a frantic scramble as if in a pinball machine. Both Rakesh and Kerry had efforts blocked before the ball fell invitingly at the feet of the goalkeeper – Danebridge's keeper.

Mark thundered his shot past the helpless Brentway goalie and leapt into the air with delight. It was his first goal of the season. It also gave his team an amazing 10-1 victory.

'This is the best kind of big win!'

Chris cried in excitement. 'Something money just can't buy!'

'Dead right,' Mark agreed happily. 'A nice round number like ten is better than square numbers any day!'

THE END